T0419388

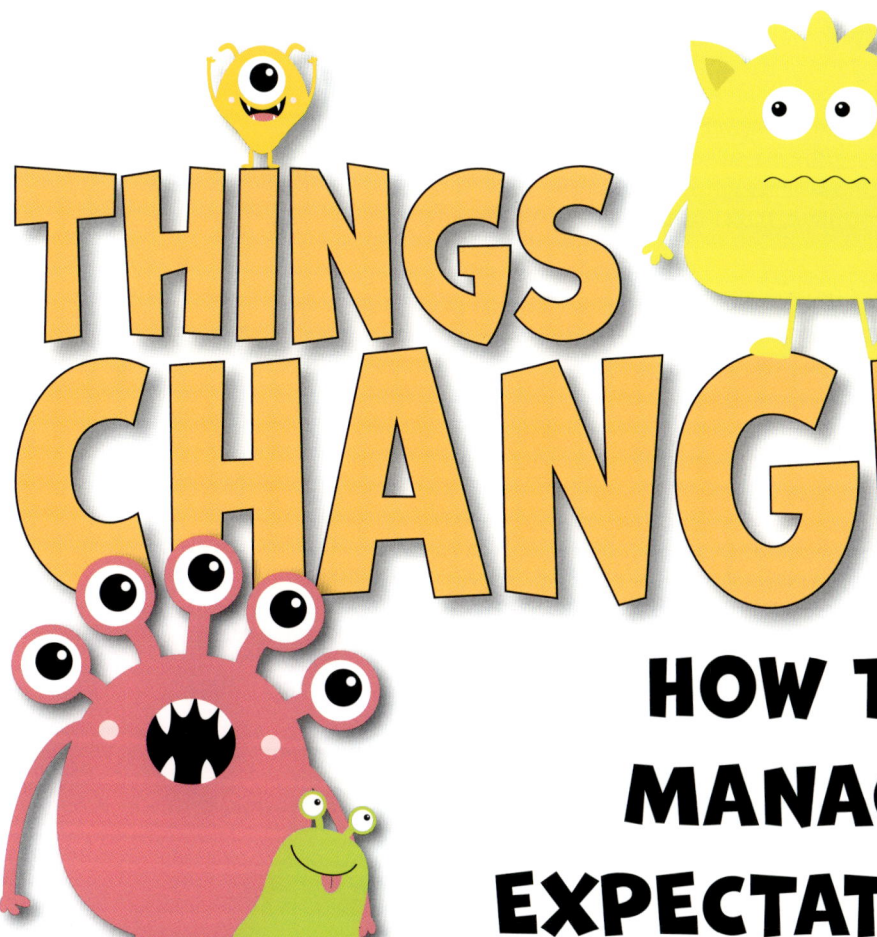

THINGS CHANGE

HOW TO MANAGE EXPECTATIONS

by Mari Schuh

BEARPORT PUBLISHING

Minneapolis, Minnesota

Library of Congress Cataloging-in-Publication Data

Names: Schuh, Mari C., 1975- author.
Title: Things change : how to manage expectations / by Mari Schuh.
Description: Fusion books. | Minneapolis, Minnesota : Bearport Publishing Company, [2023] | Series: Life works! | Includes index.
Identifiers: LCCN 2022007002 (print) | LCCN 2022007003 (ebook) | ISBN 9781636919461 (library binding) | ISBN 9781636919522 (paperback) | ISBN 9781636919584 (ebook)
Subjects: LCSH: Adjustment (Psychology) in children--Juvenile literature. | Life change events--Juvenile literature
Classification: LCC BF723.A28 S48 2023 (print) | LCC BF723.A28 (ebook) | DDC 155.4/1824--dc23/eng/20220304
LC record available at https://lccn.loc.gov/2022007002
LC ebook record available at https://lccn.loc.gov/2022007003

CONTENTS

When Things Change 4

Always Changing 6

Big Feelings 8

From the Ground Up 10

Feel Your Feelings. 12

Practice Makes Perfect 14

Keep Your Habits 16

Staying the Same. 18

Patience. 20

Go with the Flow 22

Glossary. 24

Index 24

WHEN THINGS CHANGE

It is usually easier to do things when we know what will happen. What about when things are different? Surprise!

Changes can be hard. But we can learn how to **manage** our **expectations**. Then, changes are a little easier.

My favorite mud puddle is gone!

The sun changed it to dirt.

ALWAYS CHANGING

Changes happen all the time. They can be big or small.

A new baby in the family is a big change.

Trying something new to eat is a change, too. It is just smaller.

6

When we know a change is coming, we can get ready for it. It can make things easier when we know what to expect.

Think about something in your life that will change. What do you expect to happen?

BIG FEELINGS

No matter how much we expect them, changes can give us big feelings. We may be excited. Sometimes, we feel **stressed** or worried.

It's normal to have big feelings when there is change. Taking a short break may help us shrink our feelings to size. We can do things to **relax!**

I listen to music to relax!

I love to go for a wiggle around the block!

FROM THE GROUND UP

Shrinking our feelings can start with relaxing our bodies.

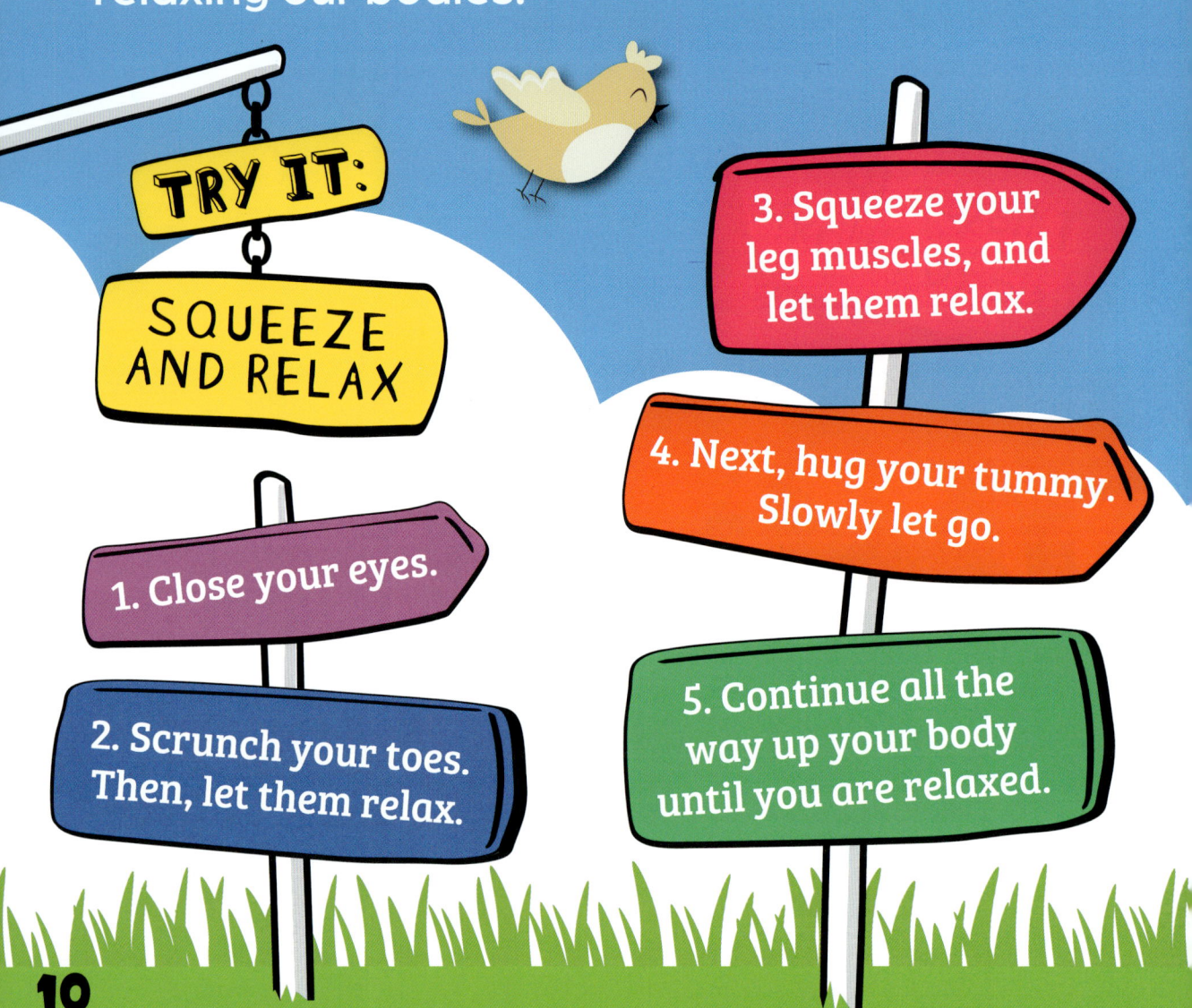

TRY IT:

SQUEEZE AND RELAX

1. Close your eyes.

2. Scrunch your toes. Then, let them relax.

3. Squeeze your leg muscles, and let them relax.

4. Next, hug your tummy. Slowly let go.

5. Continue all the way up your body until you are relaxed.

11

FEEL YOUR FEELINGS

However we feel, it's important that we let our feelings out in a healthy way. Sharing with someone we trust can help when things change. Who can we talk to?

There may be someone at home who will listen.

Maybe a teacher or someone else at school can talk with us about our feelings.

The person we share with might even have ideas about how we can deal with the change!

13

PRACTICE MAKES PERFECT

Talking about our feelings can be hard.
Get used to it by practicing with a friend.

TRY IT:

FEELING THINGS OUT

1. Get together with a buddy.

2. Pick a feeling. Don't tell your friend what it is.

3. Have them ask questions about the feeling.

4. Can your buddy guess the feeling?

Do you like feeling this way?

It's one of my favorite ways to feel!

15

KEEP YOUR HABITS

Even as some things change, others do not. We can try to keep the things we still have control over the same. That way, we know what to expect for those things.

I am moving to a new cave. But I can still brush my fur every day.

Sticking to healthy habits and **routines** helps keep some things the same. We can be sure to stay active, eat well, and get enough sleep.

STAYING THE SAME

Make a routine for bed. It can stay the same while other things change.

TRY IT:

READY FOR BED

1. Put on PJs.

2. Brush your teeth.

3. Read a story.

4. Go to sleep at the same time every night.

Shhh!

Sweet dreams!

PATIENCE

Big or small, getting used to changes can take time. Being **patient** is important. That means we stay calm no matter how long it takes.

Being patient can be easier with a friend.

We can be patient with ourselves and with others. This helps us manage things as we get used to a new normal.

Can you think of two ways you can be patient when things change?

GO WITH THE FLOW

Things are always changing. Change is the one thing we can always expect. By managing how we respond, we can make change fun!

I am full of patience.

23

GLOSSARY

expectations thoughts about what should or could happen

manage to take care of something and keep it running smoothly

patient calm even when things are difficult

relax to rest and be calm

routines regular ways of doing things in a set order

stressed nervous or worried

INDEX

calm 20

control 16

expect 5, 7–8, 16, 22

feelings 8–10, 12–15

habits 16–17

manage 5, 21

patient 20–22

relax 9–11

routines 17–18

talking 12–14